Erika the Pacifier Fairy
& the magic pacifier

By Andrea Locket

Coyright Andrea Lo9cket 2023. All rights reserved. No part of this book may be reproduced or used in any manner without the prior written permission of the copyright owner, except for the use of brief quotations in a book review.

The Frog Prince finds Erika the Pacifier Fairy

Erika casts a magic spell

The Frog Prince takes the Pacifier to baby Sammy

The spell lasts until Sammy is all grown
Then Erika visits when she is all alone
I am so pleased you have slept happily each night
It's time to give the magic back and do what's right

The Frog Prince bringing a gift from fairyland

Watch out for other Books in the Be Brave Series

Manufactured by Amazon.ca
Bolton, ON

33361983R00017